D0375069

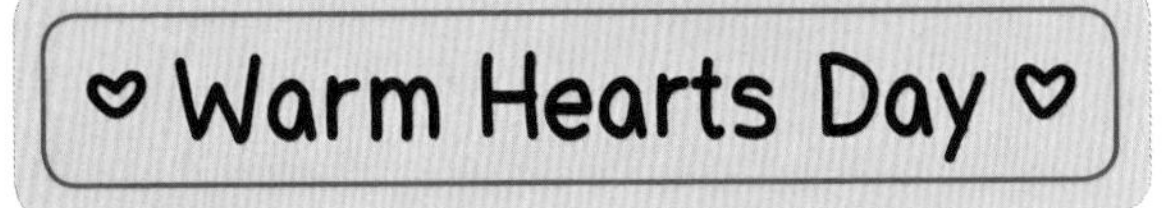
Warm Hearts Day

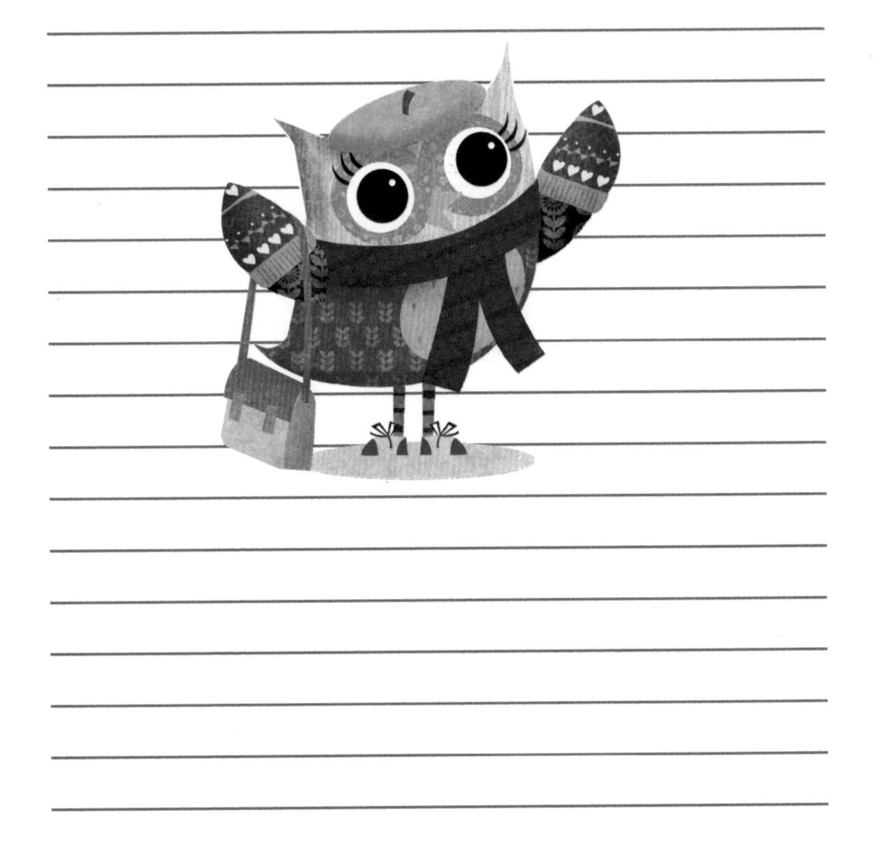

Read more
OWL DIARIES
books!
OWL DIARIES
Eva's Treetop Festival
Rebecca Elliott
SCHOLASTIC
1
OWL DIARIES
Eva Sees a Ghost
Rebecca Elliott
SCHOLASTIC
2
OWL DIARIES
A Woodland Wedding
Rebecca Elliott
SCHOLASTIC
3
OWL DIARIES
Eva and the New Owl
Rebecca Elliott
SCHOLASTIC
4
OWL DIARIES
Warm Hearts Day
Rebecca Elliott
SCHOLASTIC
5
OWL DIARIES
Baxter Is Missing
Rebecca Elliott
SCHOLASTIC
6

OWL DIARIES

♡ Warm Hearts Day ♡

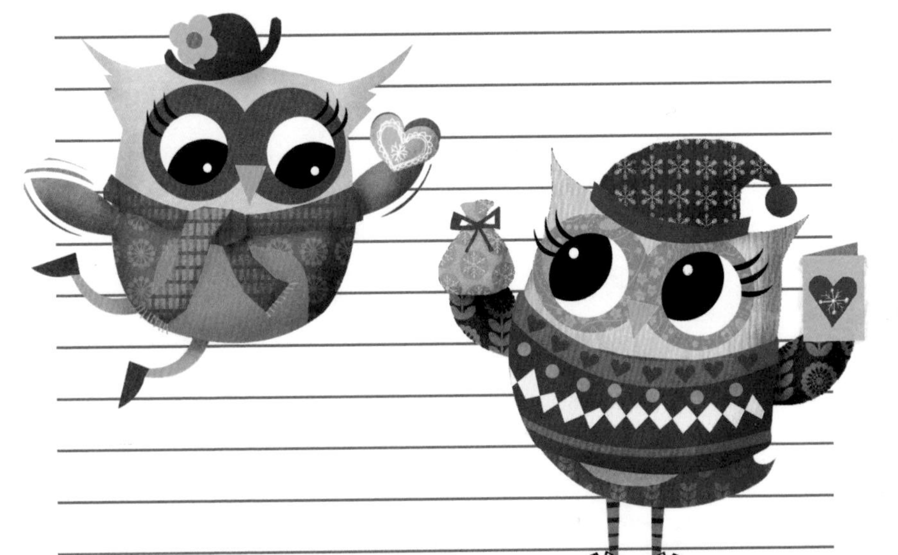

Rebecca Elliott

BRANCHES™

SCHOLASTIC INC.

For Katie and Marissa,
the wind beneath Eva's wings. —R.E.

Special thanks to Eva Montgomery.

Library of Congress Cataloging-in-Publication Data

Names: Elliott, Rebecca, author. | Elliott, Rebecca. Owl diaries ; 5.
Title: Warm Hearts Day / Rebecca Elliott.
Description: First edition. | New York : Branches/Scholastic Inc., 2016. | Series: Owl diaries ; 5 | Summary: Warm Hearts Day is approaching and Eva has been making lots of fun gifts and treats for her friends, but as the big party at the Old Oak Tree nears, she realizes that she has neglected to make any gifts for her family.
Identifiers: LCCN 2016019783| ISBN 9781338042801 (pbk.) | ISBN 9781338042818 (hardcover)
Subjects: LCSH: Owls—Juvenile fiction. | Holidays—Juvenile fiction. | Gifts—Juvenile fiction. | Friendship—Juvenile fiction. | CYAC: Holidays—Fiction. | Gifts—Fiction. | Owls—Fiction. | Friendship—Fiction.
Classification: LCC PZ7.E45812 War 2016 | DDC [Fic]—dc23 LC record available at https://lccn.loc.gov/2016019783

ISBN 978-1-338-04281-8 (hardcover) / ISBN 978-1-338-04280-1 (paperback)

10 9 8 7 6 5 4 3 2 1 16 17 18 19 20

Printed in Malaysia 108
First edition, November 2016

Book design by Marissa Asuncion
Edited by Katie Carella

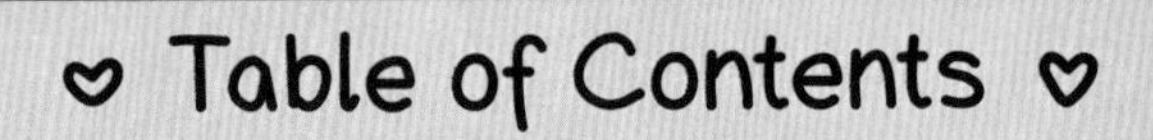

♡ Table of Contents ♡

11

1 Here I Am!

Sunday

Hello Diary,

It's Eva Wingdale here! This is going to be a **WING-TASTIC** week! I am really in the holiday mood!

I love:

Snow

My brother Humphrey's band

HOOTLES

The word "spoon"

My leaf collection

Winter sweaters

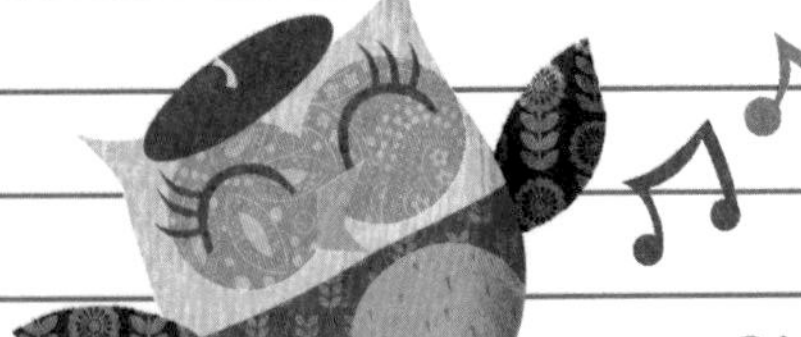

Singing loudly

Warm Hearts Day
(I'll tell you all about
it soon, Diary!)

Warm
Hearts
Day

Giving
presents

I DO NOT love:

Bright sunshine

Humphrey coming into my room WITHOUT KNOCKING

Feeling embarrassed

Sweeping snow

Mom's beetle burgers

The word "splat"

My alarm clock

Forgetting things

But I DO really love my family!

Here is a picture of us sledding:

Dad
Mom
Me
Humphrey
Baby Mo

I TOTALLY love my pet bat, Baxter, too!

Here he is dressed as a snowman:

It's **OWLMAZING** being an owl!

We stay awake ALL night.

We sleep ALL day.

And we live in tree houses in the forest.

My best friend, Lucy, lives next door at number 9. We talk on our **PINEPHONES** a lot.

We both go to school at Treetop Owlementary.

Here is our class photo:

Mrs. Featherbottom
Zac
Macy
Kiera
Carlos
Sue
Hailey
Lilly
Lucy
Me
Jacob
George
Zara

Oh, Diary, I haven't told you about WARM HEARTS DAY yet! (I can be super forgetful!) It is the most **FLAPPY-FABULOUS** holiday in Treetopolis!

All of the animals in the forest decorate their houses.

We give one another cards and presents.

We eat great food!

We even have a big party at the Old Oak Tree!

Hootles

The fun begins tomorrow because Warm Hearts Day is next Saturday! Good-day, Diary!

♡Frozen Feathers and Fur♡

Monday

I flew to school with Lucy tonight.

Wow, Lucy! Your bag looks owlmazing!
Thanks, Eva! I decorated it with Warm Hearts Day symbols: hearts, snowflakes, and music notes.
I love it! I'll decorate my bag after school!
Yay! Then we'll have matching bags!

Everyone was excited at school tonight. Only five days to go!

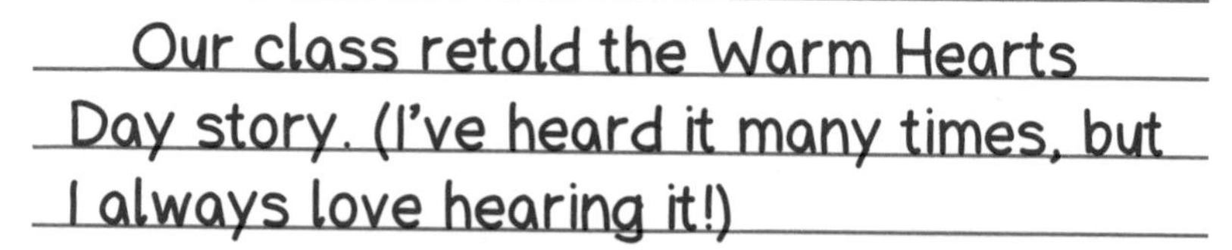

Our class retold the Warm Hearts Day story. (I've heard it many times, but I always love hearing it!)

A long time ago, all the animals of the forest fought with one another. Everyone was angry and sad.

One day, there was a terrible snowstorm. A fairy called Twinklewings fell into the forest on a snowflake.

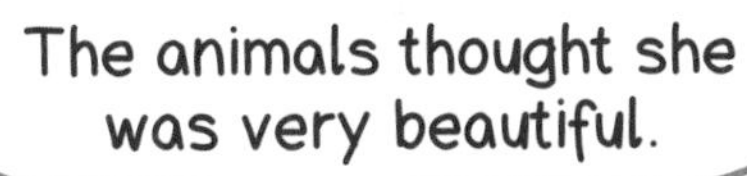
The animals thought she was very beautiful.

Twinklewings asked the animals for help. She told them she had fallen because it was too cold for her wings to work. The only way for her to get home was if the animals' hearts were warm enough to carry her there.

The animals wanted to help the fairy. So they stopped fighting and became friends instead.

They sang a song of friendship, called "Frozen Feathers and Fur." Twinklewings rode the music back up to Fairyland!

Mrs. Featherbottom flew up front.

Every winter, we get together on Warm Hearts Day to celebrate Twinklewings's journey home, and to remember how important it is to be kind to one another.

She said something **EGG-CITING** next . . .

Mr. Swoopstone, the mayor of Treetopolis, has chosen our class to sing the special Warm Hearts Day song at the party on Saturday! We will practice the song all week, make costumes, and learn dance moves.
YAY!
YAY!

After school, I made this Warm Hearts Day garland.

I'm going to use it to decorate my bag. Lucy will be happy to see my matching bag! (And I like making my friends happy!)

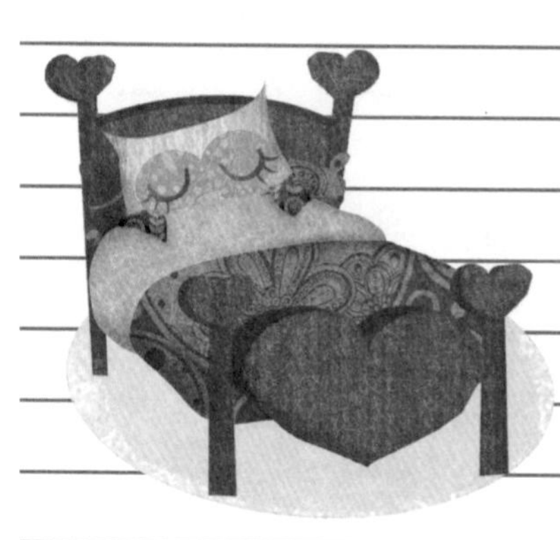

I'd better get to sleep. I need to rest my voice so it sounds **HOOTIFUL** when we practice the song tomorrow!

Cards and Winter Fairies

Tuesday

On the way to school, I surprised Lucy with my new bag decorations.

Cool, Eva!
Thanks, bag-buddy!

When we got to school, Macy, Carlos, and George gave out Warm Hearts Day cards.

I'm planning to give mine out on Friday, which is Warm Hearts Day Eve. I always make my own cards. (They're more special that way!)

I asked Lucy and Hailey to come over tonight so we can work on our cards together.

I can't wait!
I'd love to!

Our class practiced the song. Singing it really puts me in the Warm Hearts Day mood! I especially love the chorus (this is the part we sing over and over):

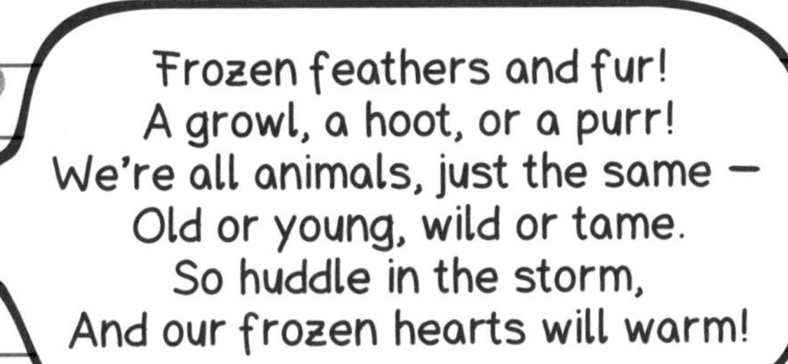
Frozen feathers and fur!
A growl, a hoot, or a purr!
We're all animals, just the same —
Old or young, wild or tame.
So huddle in the storm,
And our frozen hearts will warm!

Then Mrs. Featherbottom **HOOTED**.

We'll make costumes tomorrow, so please bring materials to make your outfit extra-special.

What should I bring, Diary?

Lucy and Hailey came over after school.

First, we played dress-up with our pets. Don't Chester, Baxter, and Rex make great Winter Fairies?

Chester
Baxter
Rex

Next, we made our cards. Don't they look great?

It was time for dinner. So Lucy and Hailey flew home. Mom made my favorite – tree slime pie!

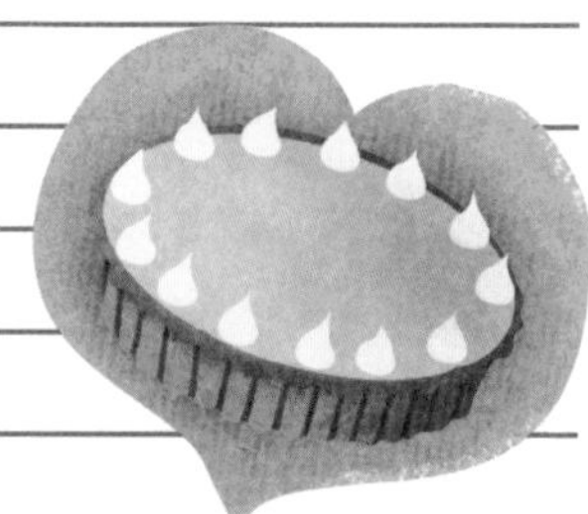

Then I wrote a list of everything I need to bring to school tomorrow.

Costume Stuff for School:
Pink and red ribbons
Felt hearts
Red shirt
Snowflake fabric
Shiny snowflake stickers
Glitter stars
Sequins
Cotton balls

Oh my! This is quite a lot of stuff. I hope I can carry it all!

♡ Warm Cookie Hearts ♡

Wednesday

It wasn't easy flying to school tonight! My bag of costume stuff was SO heavy that it kept dragging me down to the ground!

Lilly gave out heart-shaped cookies at school.

These are YUMMY, Lilly!
Thank you, Eva!

Lilly's cookies were so good that I've decided to bake holiday cookies, too!

Kiera and Lucy are going to help me after school today!

Our class got right to work on our costumes for the big song.

Your costume looks great, Eva! It's almost as nice as mine.
Thanks, Sue!

I love that around Warm Hearts Day EVERYONE is nice – even Sue! I used to call her Meany McMeanerson but, this week, I will call her Nicey McLovely.

Nicey
McLovely
100555

Lucy, Kiera, and I practiced our song on the way home. I got SO into the music that I crashed into a tree!

Luckily, no one saw
me – except for my friends.
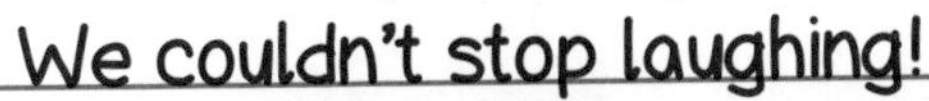
We couldn't stop laughing!

When we got to my house, Mom was getting ready to fly off.

Hello, girls! Would you like to come Warm Hearts Day shopping with me?

Thanks, but I already did my shopping.

Me too.

I'm going to go shopping tomorrow night.

Can we bake cookies?

Of course, my little owlet — as long as I can have one later!

Lucy, Kiera, and I got right to work. We put chocolate, nuts, and bugs in our cookies!

Winter Crumblies Recipe
1 cup flour
1/2 cup birdseed
1/2 cup chocolate
1/4 cup walnuts
3 bugs
- Mix everything together
- Bake for 12 minutes
- Let cookies cool
- Enjoy!
Wow! These are yummy!

Mom got home just in time to taste one.

It's time for bed. I hope I dream about Twinklewings!

5 ♡ EEK! ♡

Thursday

Zara wore a **FLAP-TASTIC** Warm Hearts Day hat to school tonight. It looked so warm and cozy!

Wow! Great hat, Zara!
Thanks, Eva! I made it myself.

Zara's hat made me want to make something cozy, too! I'll get crafty after school.

In class, Mrs. Featherbottom taught us some dance moves to go with the song. (George kept tripping over his own feet. It was so funny!)

Ha Ha!

After school, I flew home as fast as my wings could carry me.

What's the rush, Eva?
I'm going to make something, and I can't wait to get started!

Look what I made, Diary!

These cozy **WING WARMERS** should keep me nice and toasty at the Warm Hearts Day party!

Then I had an idea. I called Lucy and Hailey.
Hi! Do you want to come over on Saturday, so we can get ready for the party together?
11
Yes, please! That would be flaperrific!
9
I'd love to come!
7

I was just putting the finishing touches on my **WING WARMERS** when Humphrey crashed into my room.

Hey, Eva. I've hardly seen you all week. What have you been doing?

I've been making Warm Hearts Day decorations, cards, cookies, and now — these!

You sure have been busy! I just hope you haven't been too busy to get my present. And nothing with hearts on it!

That's when I realized something, Diary. Something totally, **FEATHER-FLAPPINGLY** terrible!

Oh **SQUIRREL-PLOP**!!! I've been SO busy this week that I forgot to get presents for my family!

ARGHHHHHH!!!

Warm Hearts Day is only two days away! EEK!!

Don't worry, Diary. I have a plan. I'm going to wake up SUPER CRAZY early tomorrow – while the sun is still up. I'll find presents for my family then.

I'm hoping to find honey for Dad, flowers for Mom, an acorn that I could make into a rattle for Baby Mo, and a stick I could make into a slingshot for Humphrey.

See you bright and early, Diary!

My Daytime Adventure

Friday

My alarm went off WAY too early today. Every other owl was still asleep.

I packed my bag so that I could head right to school after finding the presents. (I can't wait to give out my cards and cookies to everyone at school tonight!) I wore my new **WING WARMERS**.

I flew outside. The sun was so bright it hurt my eyes. But the snow did look really lovely and sparkly!

I flew all over trying to find presents for my family. Then I saw three woolly sheep. They looked a bit sad.

Hello. It's almost
Warm Hearts Day!
Why are you sad?

Hello, little owl.
We just can't get into the holiday mood.
Yeah. Our barn looks like it does every other day: boring.

Eva looked at the plain barn. Then she looked at her bag.

Oh dear. Well, I have these decorations . . . You could use them to make your barn look special. Would that help?

Yes! Thank you!
Your decorations look baa-utiful!
Happy Warm Hearts Day!

I flew around the fields in a flap. I had to find presents soon, or I'd be late for school!

Then I saw a family of beavers. They looked worried.

Hello, beavers. What's the matter?

Oh, hello, little owl. We're just finding it hard to have warm hearts today because our little ones are freezing.
We're worried they won't be able to enjoy the holiday tomorrow.

I looked down at my cozy **WING WARMERS**. They looked good on me. But they would really warm up those little beavers.

I have just the thing to warm up your holiday! Here — take my wing warmers. Maybe the twins can wear them as hats?

Wow! That's gnaw-fully kind of you!
Happy Warm Hearts Day!

I needed to hurry up and find some presents! But next, I saw three bears. They looked down in the dumps – just like the sheep.

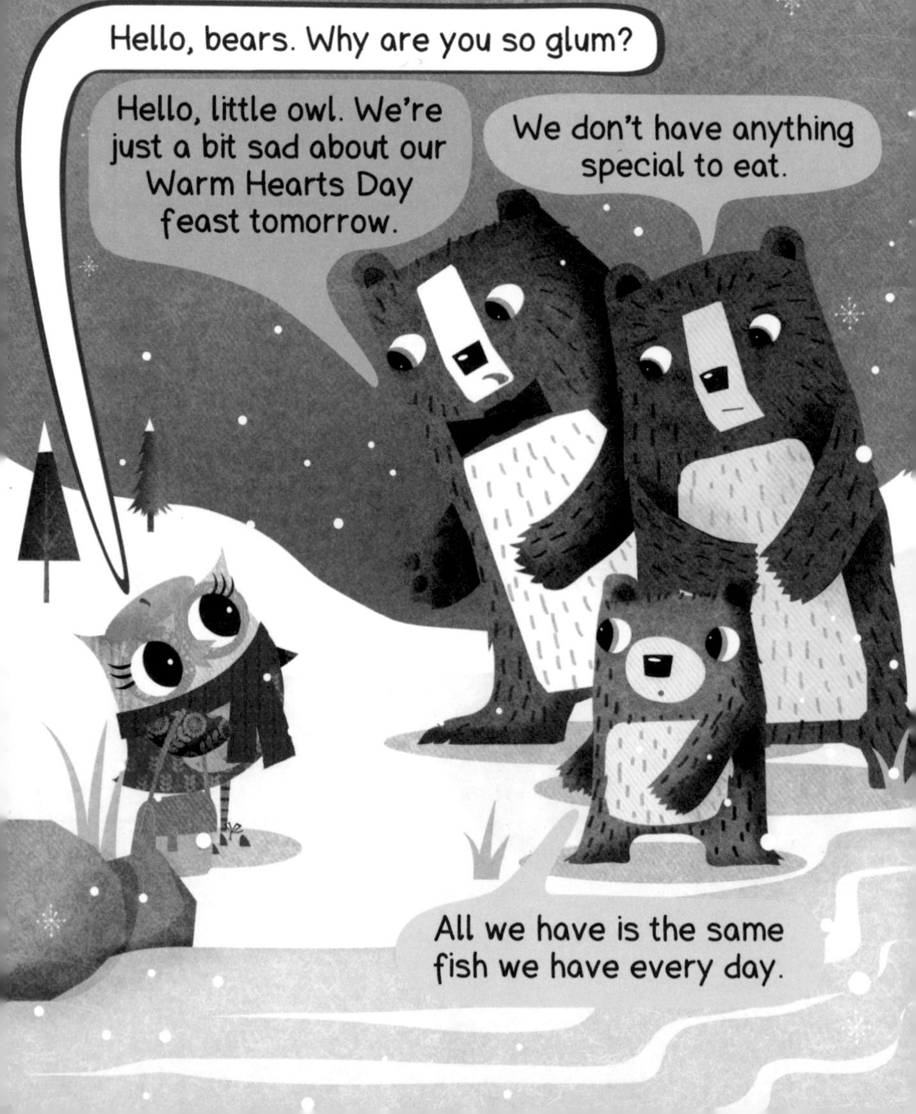

Hello, bears. Why are you so glum?

Hello, little owl. We're just a bit sad about our Warm Hearts Day feast tomorrow.

We don't have anything special to eat.

All we have is the same fish we have every day.

I knew just what would help!

Here! Please eat these Winter Crumblies at your feast. I made them myself!

Wow! That's bear-illiant!
Happy Warm Hearts Day!

Oh no! The moon was out! I was happy to help the sheep, the beavers, and the bears. But I ran out of time to find presents for my family — and I was so tired. Time for school, Diary . . .

We all gave out our cards.

Then some owls gave out cookies. I didn't have mine to give out anymore.

I felt a bit bad because I know everyone would have loved my cookies.

I couldn't stop yawning at lunch.

Why are you so tired, Eva?
And why didn't you bring in the cookies we baked?
It's a long story. And I'm too tired to tell it right now. But are you still coming over tomorrow to get ready for the party?
I can't wait!
Me too!

Soon it was time for singing practice. Diary, something <u>totally</u> <u>terrible</u> happened!

We started singing and then I FELL ASLEEP IN THE MIDDLE OF THE SONG!!!

Z
ZZZ

Lucy woke me up, but everyone was staring and laughing. It was funny but also SO EMBARRASSING!

As soon as Mrs. Featherbottom rang Barry the Bell, I flew home. I wanted to hurry so I could still try to make presents for my family. But, right away, Mom saw how tired I was. (Moms see everything!)

You have to get some rest, darling. Otherwise, you won't enjoy Warm Hearts Day tomorrow.

So, I'm in bed, Diary. But I think I should get up and make those presents. I'm . . . just . . . so . . . tired . . . I . . . want . . . to . . . slee . . .

♡Happy Warm Hearts Day!♡

Saturday

I was woken up by Lucy and Hailey bursting through my bedroom door.

Yay! It's Warm Hearts Day!
Happy Warm Hearts Day, Eva!
Oh no! I slept through my alarm! Um . . . Happy Warm Hearts Day.

I tried to sound happy. But I felt bad because I didn't have any presents for my family.

What's wrong, Eva?

I didn't get my family any presents. I was so busy making things for my friends, I forgot all about my family!
Maybe you could give them the cookies we made?
I gave those away to help some animals. And my wing warmers and bag decorations are gone, too.
That sounds very kind of you, Eva. Don't worry. I'm sure your family won't mind.
They know you love them even without presents.

Come on, Eva. Let's get dressed. That'll make you feel better!
Then we can practice the song again!

We put on our costumes.

We sang the song.

We looked and sounded pretty good. But I only felt a tiny bit better. Then Lucy and Hailey flew home to meet up with their families.

11
Bye, Eva!
See you soon at the party!

Grandpa Owlfred and Granny Owlberta came over. They loved my costume!

Then it was time to leave for the party. My family flew there together. (Oh, Diary, I felt so bad going empty-winged!)

Excited owls filled every branch of the Old Oak Tree. Mr. Swoopstone stepped up to the microphone.
Welcome to our Warm Hearts Day celebration! To start things off, Mrs. Featherbottom's class is going to sing "Frozen Feathers and Fur."

We were all excited to sing and dance in front of everyone. My tummy felt like it was tumbling around under my feathers!

When we finished, everybody cheered! It was **FLAP-TASTIC**!

But soon I felt sad again. It was time for families to exchange presents.

I'm so sorry. I don't have presents for any of you. I've let you all down . . .
That's okay, Eva. Remember the true meaning of Warm Hearts Day?
Presents, surprises, and food?!

Today is all about being kind and helping others. Twinklewings the Winter Fairy didn't bring anyone presents. Her heart was so beautiful that she made everyone warm and happy just by being there. That's how you make us feel.

Thanks, Dad.

Diary, you won't believe what happened next!

The sheep, beavers, and bears I had met showed up at the Old Oak Tree!

Everyone went quiet as a sheep started bleating down below.

We would like to wish everyone a very happy Warm Hearts Day — especially one very special little owl. Her kindness reminded us what Warm Hearts Day is all about. In return, we have made wool sweaters for everyone.

Next, a beaver started talking.

We would like to thank that same little owl for keeping our little ones warm. She showed us what Warm Hearts Day is all about. As a thank-you, we have made wooden toys for everyone.

Everyone clapped. My cheeks turned bright red.

Then a bear spoke up!

This little owl's kindness reminded us, too, of the true meaning of Warm Hearts Day. She is like a real Winter Fairy! So, to thank her, we have brought fresh fish for everyone to eat!

Lucy's and Hailey's mouths dropped open. Everyone looked up at me and cheered. The sheep, beavers, and bears smiled.

So that's where the cookies went!
Eva is the "little owl"!

I'm so proud of you, my little twinkle wings.
You are full of surprises after all!

Then everyone lifted me up in the air.
Let's all raise a glass to Eva — for being such a generous and kind Winter Fairy-owl!

The sheep, beavers, and bears shared their presents with everyone. We had the best Warm Hearts Day ever!

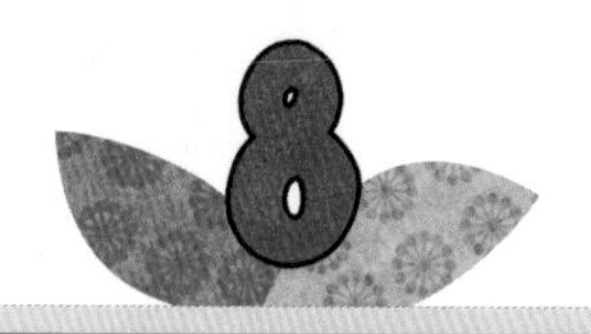

♡ Let's Keep the Party Going! ♡

Sunday

Hi Diary,

What a night it was! Guess what – the party is still going! It has been SO much fun that nobody wanted to go home!

The band is still playing.
THE HOOTLES
The food keeps coming.
The acorn syrup
still tastes sweet.
And Grandpa Owlfred
is still dancing!

Everybody was in a **WING-TASTIC** mood! It was like Twinklewings came and sprinkled Warm Hearts Day fairy dust on everyone!

But it is not fairies who make everything feel magical and lovely. It's us – and the special creatures all around us.

See you next time, Diary. Oh, and Happy Warm Hearts Day!

Rebecca Elliott was a lot like Eva when she was younger: She loved making things and hanging out with her best friends. Now that Rebecca is older, not much has changed — except that her best friends are her husband, Matthew, and their children. She still loves making things, like stories, cakes, music, and paintings. But as much as she and Eva have in common, Rebecca cannot fly or turn her head all the way around. No matter how hard she tries.

Rebecca is the author of JUST BECAUSE and MR. SUPER POOPY PANTS. OWL DIARIES is her first early chapter book series.

OWL DIARIES

How much do you know about Warm Hearts Day?

How do Eva and the other animals in the forest celebrate Warm Hearts Day?

What is the story of Warm Hearts Day?

What does Eva do with her homemade decorations, wing warmers, and cookies?

The author combines English words with words related to an animal. For example, the owls say hootiful and the sheep say baa-utiful. What animal word and what English word make up each new word? Pick a word and an animal. Then create your own word!

Make your own Flaptastic Dictionary! In a notebook, write down all of Eva's special owl words. Then write the English words beside the owl words. And include definitions, too.